Mahogany's Folly

A Race Against Time

MW01702162

Andrea Lipscomb

Copyright © 2024
All Rights Reserved

ISBN: 979-8-89212-682-3

Dedication

To my dearest Grandma Mary Virginia and Uncle Clarence who ignited my passion for reading, the greatest gift of self-exploration I could ever receive.

Acknowledgment

I would like to express my deepest gratitude to my incredible colleagues for lending their ears and hearts to my book. To my family, a special thank you to my mother, Camberlena, my cousin Robbie, and my son, Dylan, whose love and support are the bedrock of my life.

About the Author

Andrea Lipscomb, a graduate of Virginia State University, resides in Central Virginia. With a passion for Sci-Fi and British Crime TV, she brings a unique blend of interests to her writing. Andrea's professional background encompasses social work, crisis intervention, and intellectual disabilities.

Preface

In the heart of New York, where the city's pulse echoes through its streets, unfolds a tale of the clandestine world of shadows and crime, where the lines between right and wrong blur for the right price.

In this gripping chronicle, we follow the enigmatic and unbridled quest of Mahogany as she teeters on the edge of the law, navigating her way through the elaborate web of a life built on heists and secret endeavors. The city of New York becomes the backdrop to her exploits and becomes a character in its own right – a witness to the whispers, the laughter, and the shadows that lurk in its corners.

Mahogany's journey, tangled with the lives of Vonn and Nicole, takes unexpected twists as they balance the thrill of stolen riches with the weight of the choices they make. As the cityscape closes in on them, the characters grapple with the consequences of their actions, their destinies shaped by the streets they call home.

This preface invites you to traverse narrow alleys and bustling salons, where every decision carries a price, and every shadow hides a secret. Join Mahogany in her pursuit of freedom, where alliances are fragile, and the city's whispers become the soundtrack to a life lived in the shadows of crime.

"*Mahogany's Folly*" beckons you to explore a world where every step leads deeper into the web of risk and reward, and freedom is an elusive prize.

Contents

Chapter 1: The Beginnings

Doctor Proctor's office was an old building between the city's busiest streets. The sign outside read 'Proctor Counseling Services.' I took a deep breath and stepped inside. A soft chime welcomed me into a waiting area.

The walls of this place were a pastel blue and exuded a sense of calm and serenity. I was greeted by Dr. Proctor's receptionist, who seemed to be working on some forms when I walked in. She looked up and smiled at me warmly. We exchanged pleasantries, and then she told me that I should wait in the doctor's office.

"*He'd be in shortly,*" she said.

His office was much more cozy, like an extension of the calm waiting area. It had several shelves lined with academic books. A large, sturdy oak desk was placed against one wall with a lot of things: pens, different documents and papers, some small potted plants, and a family portrait. At the center of the room were two armchairs that faced each other, and there was a small coffee table between them.

One office wall had all the degrees and certifications that Dr. P had earned. The rest of them were adorned with paintings and quotes. One corner of the room had a window that overlooked the busy street — the light from which flooded the whole room. Sheer white curtains danced at the breeze, creating a calming effect.

I settled into one of the armchairs in the therapist's office, taking in the office's atmosphere and wondering what the session would be like. I turned my attention to my fingers and admired my freshly painted acrylic nails. I chose a bright red and orange colored manicure this time around. They looked like little flames.

I wiggled my fingers to make the fire dance and smiled - amused at the thought. A moment later, I heard a soft knock on the door, which opened to reveal Dr. Proctor. He entered the room with a kind smile. He seemed not only professional but also approachable. He wore a soft-colored shirt and beige pants.

"*Good afternoon, Mahogany,*" he said in a calming and warm voice and continued, "*I hope I didn't take too long.*"

I nodded and smiled at him. "*No problem at all.*"

He sat in the other armchair, crossed his legs, and leaned forward slightly. He seemed genuinely interested in our conversation.

"*Well, I'm glad to hear that. So, how are you feeling today? Is there something you want to talk about?*"

His open-ended question invited me to speak freely.

"*Well, Doc, to be honest with you, I, Mahogany Nicole Worthy, who is sexy with more bounce to the ounce, am a bona fide liar! I said what I said. PERIOD! Did you get that on your little tape recorder?*"

I couldn't help but taunt him. I had heard the term over and over again, and I had made peace with it. So, what? I am a liar. I'll tell him how it is. As I sat before Doctor Proctor, he peered at me with a subtle expression. It seemed that his gaze was piercing through the rim of his glasses into me.

"*Oh yes, Miss Worthy, this was recorded. I must say, you seem rather unapologetic about the lies that you tell.*"

I heaved a deep sigh, feeling the weight of disappointment settling in my chest.

"*Don't get me wrong. I feel sad when I am not invited to family functions and people putting away their good China, their good weed, and wigs. It feels like I'm not fully accepted for who I am, and it's a difficult pill to swallow*".

I replied as I brushed my fingers through my hair. I've permanently dyed it the deepest shade of mahogany, which earned me my name.

"*So, when did the love of lying start?*" Doctor Proctor asked me.

Keeping his sharp gaze on me the entire time, he ended his remark with a sizzling question. The question made me slightly uneasy, so I retorted to my usual defense mechanism — humor.

"*Wow, I really want to say once upon a time on Edsall Road in Alexandria, Virginia, but that sounds corny!*" I replied and let out a chuckle.

Dr. P appeared surprised by my remark, as though he did not anticipate me articulating my feelings in such a manner. He could discern that I derived amusement from the circumstances. It was the only way I felt empowered and in control.

"*Okay. Okay. Let's take you back to one of my early days. It was around 5 in the morning. I would pee in the bed even though I had a bathroom across from the bedroom with the light on. The urine would get all over the bed, on my sister and our beloved dog Perdy, whom I shared a bed with.*"

The statement startled Doctor Proctor, who was listening keenly to my ramblings and scribbling something into his notes. He stopped writing briefly and then continued as I started speaking again.

"*The first time, I simply blamed the dog for my blunder and got away with it quite easily. The second time my mother found the bed wet, I blamed my sister*

Brittany. Quite obviously, she got the wrath of the paddle. It was amusing how nothing she said seemed to change anybody's mind. My father believed what I said. However, somehow, I knew the same excuse would not work every time. I mean, I couldn't make the same excuses over again. They would get suspicious after a while. That is when it hit me. It was like a bulb lit up in my head, and a voice that whispered, 'Mahogany, ready, set, lie,' and so I did."

A smile spread across my face. I couldn't control it. The truth is I found the situation funny more than anything else.

"*So, how long did this facade go on?*" Doctor Proctor asked me.

He was inquisitive, but he kept his calm and composure. Even though the question was pressing, I didn't mind sharing the details of the incident with him. There was something trustworthy about his demeanor.

"*For about a year. My Columbo mother had gotten suspicious of me and how the bed kept getting wet every night. She stood by the closet to watch me at night. She saw that I was too scared of going to the bathroom because of the dark. I went back to bed and peed on it*", I replied as I stared at the floor.

Doctor Proctor nodded gently. His eyes had compassion and kindness. He gestured with his hands, signaling me to go on.

"*My mother was furious after discovering the truth about what I had done. After being exposed by her to the family, I felt humiliated and would find other ways to lie. I felt angry, as if someone had pulled the last straw. There was no holding me back then.*"

I settled back in the ash-grey chair and rested my right hand on the wooden armrest. I caught myself deep in thought, recalling the incident, what led to it, and the events that followed. Doctor Proctor gave me a moment. I knew he was waiting for me patiently to gather my thoughts. He did not even give me any more beckoning to continue speaking, not that I needed any. I was here to talk.

"*Once used my older sister's ID to sneak into a party at Champion's.*" I finally continued talking. "*There, I told Uncle August, an incredibly jealous man, that his wife was sneaking around with the bartender at Zinfandel's on King Street.*"

I looked up at my therapist after finishing what I was saying. He was looking straight at me with an indiscernible look on his face. It stressed me, and I blurted out, "*Well, there is some truth to the last statement, but I got the wrong bar due to my ear hustling.*"

I then added the following after taking a pause:

"*My uncle took me down to Zinfandel's and asked me to point out the man his wife had been seeing.*" I then proceeded to speak.

"*That day, I saw a good fight. Plus, I got to eat a free pizza and Cotton Candy without sharing any of it with my sisters. What I thought might be a heavenly day without my sisters turned out to be hell on my ass after my southern father, Dallas, found out the truth and got a hold of me!*"

I narrated the whole story to my therapist and took a deep breath. Doctor Proctor looked at me warmly and asked me:

"*So, What is the relationship with your father like?*"

"*Oh, he's my everything! Dallas Worthy is a hard-working entrepreneur who owns his blue and silver Caprice taxi fleet. He would often go against my mother to defend me.*" I replied.

My relationship with my mother is quite strained. The woman couldn't bear me because of my constant lies. She hates how close I am with Dallas and how he takes my side. It's like a rebellion in her kingdom. Everybody loves my mama. She is a caramel-skinned lady with the smile of Nancy Wilson and the charisma of Eartha Kitt. When she's around, everybody has their act together. Well, everybody other than me, of course. Naturally, we don't get along.

"*Dad would often tell the old bird that she was giving me a hard time. I said to Dr. Proctor. 'He would tell her that I was just embellishing the truth. He even went as far as to say, 'People in the South do that all the time, Belle!' But my mother, Belle, was a Yankee. The rules of lying were much different for her. You would end up in the alley, beaten up or killed.*"

"*Maybe she was worried about you believing in lies?*" Doctor Proctor intervened and muttered a statement in a low voice, posing it more like a question.

Right after saying that, he realized something and added it to his statement: "*That's the most dangerous thing, you know, to be a person who believes the false reality that they have made for themselves and sometimes others.*"

However, I shared a different perception than Doctor Proctor.

"*Hey! But what is wrong with a harmless imagination? What can be wrong with giving people what they want? What is so incorrect about faking it until you make it?*" I protested.

"*A whole lot, Mahogany.*" He replied in his calm and composed voice. "*People can get hurt by lies you tell. You have hurt others, right?*" Doctor Proctor ended his statement with a question.

"*Yes, I have. But in the beginning, I thought it was for their good. I was wrong for that part, maybe. All right! Alright! Don't ask about that too much now.*" I replied in defense.

Dr. Proctor smiled subtly.

"*Well. Well. Finally, Doctor Proctor smiles! Now, it looks like we are getting somewhere.*" I remarked as a joke, which turned that subtle smile into a rather obvious one.

"*To put the chocolate icing on the cake, I am my father's favorite. One reason can be that I look like his mother. Plus, I must add that I am an adventurous soul. My father always had to choose discipline over pleasure, as he was the one everyone relied on. As a result, he didn't experience the world as he wanted to. He wants me to have my experiences because he couldn't. Hence, we connect on that level.*" I told Dr Proctor.

I glanced at the wall clock, and it caught my eye. It had a beautiful wooden frame with intricate gold numerals over a pearl-white base dial. It was the prettiest wall clock I had ever seen.

My therapy session lasted for about thirty minutes. Doctor Proctor stopped me in my tracks about all the lies I had told to people. He said that the next step was confronting the lies. I had to tell everyone all that I had lied about. It is the first step to making things right.

"See you next week, Miss Worthy!" Doctor Proctor said with a warm smile on his face.

I smiled back and said, "See you, Doc."

I walked toward the door, stopped momentarily to wave at Dr. Proctor, and stepped out of his office.

Chapter 2: Meet The M Team

After spilling my guts to my therapist, I called my best friend Nicole to dish out the details of the session. I knew she would want to know how it went. Nicole is just as attractive as I am, and one thing I absolutely love is her talkative personality. She has no filter like me and is the kind of person who can cuss anybody before they can count to two. We're like two peas in a pod.

But beyond her feisty personality, she is a trustworthy friend whom I can always rely on, especially when it comes to bailing me out of crazy situations. I often get into trouble with my mother and sisters, and Nicole always helps me.

Some time back, I stole my sister Monica's tax refund money, and she found out. I desperately needed a place to crash, and Nicole came to my rescue. She offered me her place and hid me from my sister till the matter settled down. We've been inseparable ever since.

Truth be told, Nicole is as adventurous as I am. Last year, she had nothing nice to wear to her birthday party, so she stole $1000 worth of nice clothes from the mall. It was a close call, but she got away with it, and we laughed about it later.

And let's not forget the time when I went out with another guy behind my boyfriend Vonn's back. Nicole lied on my behalf to Vonn and my family while I was out with this other guy at Buffalo Wild Wings.

I know she's got my back, no matter what. We have a shared love of partying. Nicole loves to get people together, and boy, she hosts some fun parties. I remember Vonn and I had just started seeing each other when Nicole invited him to a Super Bowl party and introduced him to some people from the community.

The night was perfect; it had everything a good party has - chilled beer, good food, and great company. Vonn ended up crashing on Nicole's couch because she took his keys and wouldn't let him leave till the very end. There isn't a dull moment when she's around.

We partied all night, and Vonn later told me he had a great time. Some call him my minion jokingly, insinuating that he only sees things my way, which isn't entirely false, but I like to call him the love of my life. Of course, they could also be calling him my minion because he is short.

But he's pretty gifted where size matters. He is a textbook New Yorker who is blessed with the most gorgeous tan complexion and smoothest skin you may have ever seen. I have always hated how effortlessly beautiful his skin is. But it isn't just his looks; Vonn has unwavering self-confidence and is fiercely loyal. These things make him irresistible.

And when it comes to me, he's always on my side, seeing things the way I see them. It's like having someone with a twin mindset as if it's us against the world. I guess this is why people think he is my minion. Also, Vonn and I rarely fight, which my friends find unbelievable.

You see, the thing is that when you have found the right person, it is peaceful like that. I suppose if we ever fought or broke up, Carmen would mess him up. If you're guessing who she is, then she's my other best friend — my other guardian angel.

Carmen invented the mantra '*fuck him up*!'. She's a real firecracker and so unapologetically herself. She doesn't believe in crying over a breakup. Instead, she would relish in hatching a revenge plan to mess the other person up.

There is absolutely no taming her. She is as wild as they get. When I broke up with my ex, she told me to "put him in a cast," which left me in fits of laughter. Sometimes, conversing with her is my favorite part of my day, especially when I've had a tough day.

She has a refreshing and occasionally disturbing but amusing outlook on life — enough to uplift my spirits. Sometimes, it's hard to believe that she has firm faith in the existence of aliens and several conspiracy theories like that of Area 51 or the one that claims Elvis is still alive. Good lord!

Unlike us — Nicole, Vonn, and I — Carmen essentially likes to stay out of trouble or an '*adventure,*' as we like to call it. She'll dabble into smoking some weed occasionally, but that's about as far as she goes. Thinking of trouble and adventures, there's something big going on tonight that has my heart in knots.

Vonn and I have been staking out this local entertainer named DJ Element for the past few days. Element has been in the business since the late eighties, and he is one rich fella. He has this elegant townhouse on the Potomac, the fanciest cars, yellow and white diamond chains, and rings that I badly want.

Oh, and how can I forget the stacks of cash he shows off in his autographed pictures? He seems reasonable for the picking, but we are not sure if he keeps any money in the house. It's still worth a shot, though; we could make a fortune on the darned diamond jewelry he is always wearing.

I know I am recovering with a penchant for a bit of thievery, but Vonn has me convinced that this will be our last caper, and I believe him. The thing is that we are clearly strapped for money! This bust would really help me with my salon and Vonn with his printing business.

We can't go asking my dad for more cash anymore, especially not after the extravagant birthday bash Belle had in December. It had it all: gold and silver party ornaments everywhere and non-stop Curtis Blow and Parliament tunes blasting through the night. Gaudy — That's my mother's style. So, this robbery is the last resort.

For any successful heist, one needs to successfully stake out the target, which means observing the in and out timings for at least two days before the "bitch, give me the money" episode occurs on the third day. That had been our practice till now, but I'm hoping this is the last time we have to do that.

Vonn and I see this as an adult field trip. We are going to eat hot wings and drink Mickey's. Plus, we will use our night-vision goggles from the military surplus store to keep an eye on our target at night. Vonn uses his grandpa's car for these stakeouts, which is a plush 4-door black Buick with burgundy leather seats. Vonn said that this dude is as straight as they come.

We strategically chose a Monday night for the robbery as he has no visitors on the first two days of the week. Tonight, it all goes down.

***

"*Vonn, let me see what is going on!*" Vonn and I were parked behind several bushes the street down his townhouse. Vonn and I hid as soon as we saw a car approaching. I jerked the night goggles out of his hand and pointed them toward the open window.

"*Where are yours, Mahogany?*" Vonn asked me.

"*Well, I kind of forgot mine,*" I admitted.

"*This fool is about to pay to get laid,*" Vonn said. "*Let me see.*" He observed as DJ Element moved towards his safe and entered his password, "Write this down, Babe. Five right, nine left, 28 right, and 41 left."

I wrote this information on the small notepad I had taken out from my backpack.

"*Well, look at that! God!*" Vonn smiled. There was plenty of dough in his safe.

"*Please don't put the Lord in what we are about to do. Are we going to do this or what, Vonn?*" I asked.

"*Yes, babe, I am going to kick the door in at the count of five,*" Vonn replied.

"*No! I have a better idea. Let the DJ wine and dine this tramp; we'll strike when he takes her up to the bedroom, and they are at their most vulnerable. That shall be the moment when we will get our money.*" I answered him.

"*Good idea, babe! That's why I keep you around.*" He laughed and kissed me.

That prick Element had loud mid-tempo music on, leading the lady to the upstairs of his townhouse. He was probably telling this woman all kinds of lies. It is all in the perverted look men give, and he was doing a little slow bop and tilt with his head.

"*Yep, he's going for their draws.*" I laughed. Vonn was getting impatient at this point.

"*Mahogany, are they naked yet?*" Vonn asked.

"*Here, look for yourself!*"

"*Well. Well. Well.*" Vonn got his 9-millimeter out and said, "*Let's show Mr. Earth, Wind, Water, and Fire what time it is.*"

***

Vonn and I broke into DJ Element's house. He was upstairs having the time of his life — with music blasting through the speakers and a girl in his arms. He was unaware of what was going to happen to him. The door opened into the downstairs hall, with several glass bottles scattered on the floor, and the room reeked of alcohol and weed.

"*I bet he will be ranting a lot once he finds out about losing all his riches,*" I commented. Vonn signaled me to keep quiet and find whatever I could quickly.

The elegant townhouse on the Potomac was as dull from the inside as it could be. It was full of clutter in the form of multiple posters of eighties DJs and old ragged props — reeking of abandonment. The furniture was ancient but not antique, so it didn't possess any value. The structure was so forsaken that no one would even spend a penny on it. I walked toward a small room, assuming it might have a locker with riches inside.

I tripped over something and came crashing onto the ground with a loud bang. It took me a moment to regain my senses, but as I looked up, I saw the DJ standing right in front of me. His gigantic figure overshadowed me. I knew I had to think quickly; otherwise, it would have ended quite badly for me.

I kicked Element's leg, causing him to trip, and jumped on his back, hitting him repeatedly on the head. He slung me around while screaming in pain, and I fell after giving a final punch to his eyes, which left him crying. I ran down the hall out the back door onto the dark road while splatting and falling all over the place.

After running what seemed like a marathon, my eyes were blinded by a bright light. The next thing I knew, it felt like I hit a wall, and everything went black.

***

I opened my eyes and felt a sharp pain pulsating through my head. I realized that I had been hit by a car, and it made me hit my head hard on the concrete. I extended my arm to reach my bookbag, which had the cash that Vonn and I had stolen from the DJ's house, but it was simply too far.

We were going to take different exits and meet later near North Windsor, but that was before the robbery went up in smoke, and I fell. I didn't know how long I was out, but Vonn must have been losing his shit while waiting for me at the meeting point. I tried to straighten my legs to get up, but they gave out.

The car door sprung open, and I heard footsteps heading towards me.

"*Is she dead?*" a woman said in her high-pitched, squeaky voice that was filled with horror.

"*Let me see.*", a thick, raspy male voice replied. "*Well. Well. Well, if it isn't lying ass Mahogany!*"

I tried to look up to get a look at their faces and recognized them immediately. It was Brian and Aminata.

"*Oh, the Lord really does listen. I don't remember how long I have been meaning to get my hands on her. Hurry up and put her in the backseat before she wakes up!*" Aminata replied.

Aminata used to be a stylist at my salon until I fired her and started a battle of wits. She just had too many accidents with the scissors and over-processed one client's hair to the point that it fell off her head. I wouldn't have hired her in the first place if it hadn't been for Brian — her boyfriend and the manager of *Pancake Heaven* across the street from my salon.

He caught me stealing $200 worth of supplies and the secret recipe to those delicious pancakes that the restaurant was known for. He said he would let it slip if I gave his girl a job at the salon, and I caved in.

"Damn!" I thought to myself. I could not believe I was at Brian's mercy yet again! I thought all of this as I stared back at his face.

Chapter 3: Gone Missing

Vonn sat nervously in the car. His eyes were switching between the watch on his wrist and the deserted street ahead. I was late, and his anxiety was building with every passing second. He knew that I had a habit of forgetting things, but this time it felt different.

I was carrying a hefty $7,000 in my book bag after the robbery, and he couldn't shake off the uneasy feeling gnawing at him.

"*Why isn't she here yet?*" He said to himself repeatedly.

He was concerned about my safety and became worried about the money. With each passing minute, he grew more impatient, anxious, and paranoid.

"*Damn, she is probably a no-show.*" He said in a confused tone.

"*No, she wouldn't do me wrong,*" he reassured himself, trying to quell the rising doubt. "*It's just Mahogany being Mahogany, always in her own world.*"

Then something came across his mind if there was actually trouble this time. "*There is something wrong. Something must have held her back.*"

Vonn's thoughts were all over the place. "I *can't even go back to check on her; DJ Douche must have the whole police station parked in front of his house by now.*"

He nervously tapped his fingers on the steering wheel as his eyes searched for any movement on the street that could reveal my face. I had been waiting for her to show up but without any luck. After minutes turned into what seemed like hours, Vonn's mind began racing with a multitude of scenarios.

From me being caught by the authorities to getting into trouble with someone involved in the robbery, his thoughts were as dark as the night was. The mere thought of me being in danger sent shivers down his spine. Finally, he decided to call Nicole for help:

"*Maybe she had heard from Mahogany or knew where she might be, he thought, dialing Nicole's number, hoping she'd pick up quickly.*"

"*Hey, it's Vonn,*" he said as Nicole answered the call. "*I need your help. Mahogany's in a bit of a fix, and I can't find her.*"

"*Well, where the hell are you?*" Nicole demanded in the usual annoyed tone she had while talking to him.

"*North Windsor Road,*" Vonn replied.

"*What the hell are you doing across town? Why can't you give her a ride back?*" Nicole asked, growing more upset.

"*Just pick her up, okay?*" Vonn replied, trying to keep his voice steady despite the anxiety bubbling inside him. "*I'll leave the details for M to tell you. I don't have time to talk right now.*"

"*Did he really cut the line like that? Who does he think he is?*" Nicole thought to herself. She continued:

"*I swear if it weren't for Mahogany, I wouldn't have put up with his ass. Mahogany. I need to get to her quickly - only the Lord knows what she has gotten herself into now.*"

Nicole approached DJ Element's house in the Potomac Townhouses, and her jaw dropped in shock. The scene was filled with police cars and officers bustling around while Element and his club fly stood on the side of the home, looking like hell.

Cautiously, Nicole drove by slowly, taking in the chaotic sight before her, trying not to draw too much attention to herself.

"*Oh, hell no!*" she muttered under her breath, feeling a mix of worry and frustration. "These fools stuck up DJ Element? Damn! Vonn and Mahogany, I need compensation for this mess. I work with this prick's father."

Her anger simmered as she realized Vonn and Mahogany hadn't told her about their plans. Nicole took deep breaths, trying to calm herself, but she couldn't help but feel furious at being left in the dark. It wasn't fair to send her into their mess without knowing what lies ahead after not telling her anything about their endeavors.

"*I am going to kick my size eight shoe so deep into their behind,*" she vowed, her voice seething with anger. "*Both of them will be walking with a limp!*"

She circled Element's house for an hour, waiting for a glimpse of Mahogany, but she was nowhere to be seen.

“ *Where are you, M?*” she thought to herself.

"*Old friend, you are on your own.*" she finally muttered, feeling helpless.

Nicole dreaded calling Vonn, considering Mahogany was his everything, but she did it anyway. The mess was beyond her, and there was nothing else she could do.

“ *The fool is not here!*" Nicole yelled out with all her frustration and anger in that one sentence.

"*Damn, do you know cell phone etiquette? I think the aliens on Mars heard your ass,*" Vonn replied, distancing the phone from his ears which were hurting because of how loud Nicole had screamed.

" *This is serious now, Vonn. It has been a couple of hours now. Element's place is swimming with cops, and Mahogany is nowhere to be seen. It's time to call Big Daddy Dallas.*" Nicole explained in a calm voice, trying to get through to him.

"*I was dreading this,*" Vonn responded in a severe voice, hanging up.

His hands trembled slightly as he dialed Dallas's number, knowing he could be a force to be reckoned with. The weight of the situation weighed heavily on him, and he could only hope that Mahogany would be safe and that Dallas would help them navigate the trouble they had gotten themselves into.

He finally dialed the number, waiting for Mahogany's father to pick up.

"*Hello?*" Dallas picked up the phone after a couple of rings.

"*Huh. Mr. Worthy, guess what?*" Vonn said hesitantly.

"*Oh, damn, what have you done now?*" he asked.

"No sir, I haven't done anything. Umm. Mahogany never came to the car after a party at DJ Fire's house. Of course, my baby lied to me." Vonn lied. *Well, I can't tell him about the robbery,* he thought to himself.

" *Vonn, I will call the authorities,* "Mr. Worthy said to Vonn's horror.

Vonn said, "*I don't think it's necessary, sir. I just thought we could—*"

"*Save me the explanation; it's of no use here. I better get my daughter back safe and sound, Vonn, or you're in deep trouble.*"

Dallas' heart started pounding in his chest as he made the distressing call to 911, desperate to locate his daughter.

"*Hello, this is 911. How may I help you?*" a representative picked up the call and replied calmly.

"*This is Dallas Worthy. I need to file a missing persons report for my daughter, Mahogany. She disappeared from a party at DJ Element's house last night,*" Dallas said, trying to keep his voice steady. Hence, the operator understood him despite being consumed by a gnawing worry for his daughter's safety.

The operator's tone turned more serious. "*How old is your daughter, sir?*" He inquired.

"She's 25, around 5'4" tall, and weighs about 140 pounds," Dallas replied, providing every detail he could think of at the top of his head.

"Thank you for the valuable information, Mr. Worthy. A car will be dispatched to your home shortly. However, please be aware that the police cannot take immediate action until a full day has *passed since her disappearance, given that she is an adult*," the operator explained the standard operating procedure calmly.

"*Thanks for the encouraging words,*" Dallas said with extreme annoyance. He couldn't bear the thought of waiting an entire day while his daughter was missing.

"*By the way,*" Dallas added, trying to be as helpful as possible, "We just moved here, so not many people would know my daughter. You might want to check the Schaumberg neighborhood. She also has a salon over there."

"*Of course, I'll let the dispatched officers know this piece of information. We'll do our best to locate her.*" The operator replied in an attempt to reassure Mr. Worthy.

The waiting felt unbearable as Dallas hung up the phone. He paced anxiously, praying the police would find her safe and sound. The minutes dragged on, each feeling like an eternity, until he heard the distant sound of sirens approaching his home.

Two uniformed cops made their way through the quaint neighborhood of Schaumberg, comprising 25 tiny three-bedroom brick homes. The area exuded a sense of history; having been built in the early eighties, it had a well-manicured appearance that owed much to the unity of its residents.

The two cops made their way to the first brick home and knocked on the door. The door flung open to reveal a woman in her thirties with big hoop earrings, a thick accent, and big poofy hair.

"*Yeah, I know her. I lent her money some time back, and she hasn't returned a dime,*" the lady replied after the cop asked her if she knew Mahogany.

"*Ma'am, but have you seen her recently?*one of the cops inquired.

"*I haven't, no. But when you see her, tell that bitch she better give me my money,*" The lady replied before shutting the door in the officer's face.

"*Alright,*" the two replied unanimously before moving on to the next house.

"*What about her lying ass? Did she die?*" The following neighbor asked without a shroud of concern in his voice.

"*No, sir. She's missing. We're trying to find her.*" One of the officers replied with a serious tone.

"*Well, good luck. She's probably done someone wrong again and is hiding till it's safe to come back out.*" The thin, weary man of about forty replied.

"*Thank you for your time, sir. We'll be going now.*" The officers stated before walking off his porch.

"*That poor sweet child didn't know the truth if it gave her an ass whipping!*" remarked an older woman, shaking her head with a mix of fondness and exasperation.

"*No, she cannot live with me for the 40th time!*" a neighbor snapped, clearly exasperated with Mahogany's frequent housing requests.

"*Ma'am, we're just trying to—*" The officer's sentence was interrupted by the door that shut closed in his face.

"*Her big head messed my wig up! Tell her to replace my wig,*" another resident said, clearly frustrated.

"Mahogany? Chick didn't wash her bottom regularly! Who would want her," scoffed someone else, their comment dripping with disdain.

"*Mahogany is a loving person. She has some great stories. I could never tell when she was lying. She is a Cancer, so the ride will always be interesting.*" The testimony took aback the officers.

Finally, after a series of alarming reports, they got someone who wasn't filled with hatred for the girl. "*So, you haven't seen her, ma'am?*" The officer asked the elderly lady in a calm, gentle voice.

"*Oh, no, dear! I'm sorry I can't be of more help to you.*" She replied with evident sadness in her tone.

"*I love her salon. Always give her the correct change, or you will be $20 short.*" Another older resident on a cane gave the last statement.

"*Officer, you should have been at the salon when she fired that crazy girl with the Mohawk. I thought World War Three, Four, and Five were about to happen. A salon has too many hot things to be trying to fight*," the older lady continued.

The cops looked at each other for a brief moment and then back at the lady. They thank her for her time and walk back to their car with a notebook full of statements for Mahogany. It was clear that she was a character that left a lasting impression, one that was difficult to ignore.

Some of the town's residents may have had reasons to dislike her, while others genuinely liked her, but regardless, they couldn't easily brush her off. Mahogany's enigmatic nature and bold personality had etched her presence into the fabric of the community, leaving an indelible mark on those who knew her. Yet, no one knew her – not as much as they thought.

Chapter 4: The Kidnapping

Mahogany Wicked Worthy. Yes, my middle name is Wicked. I don't know if my mother named me that at birth or if I earned it over the years — due to my countless adventures. The truth is that I am mischievous, and I take pride in that. I've never truly understood why people see it as an unwelcoming trait. Everyone should have this attribute - it's necessary for survival and sustenance in this cruel world.

People have called me a narcissist, but I think I'm just an aesthete with an eye for beauty, and what can I do if I find myself remarkable? I'm a creative and talented soul, you see. Some time back, I wrote some verses to pay tribute to my charming personality and its many facets.

I remember reading them aloud whenever I got in trouble, as they would instantly boost my confidence.

"You can take leaps,

and you can even fly.

When you are a person

who is witty and sly."

Out of all the people, it astonishes me how I have ended up in the backseat of cars with these fools — who have all of the worst qualities. What rotten luck!

Brian and Aminata are the worst people on the planet. They are truly made for each other. It would not be kind to pair these two with anyone else. The universe found the two most rotten souls and united them.

What could be worse than being at their mercy after everything that went down? Oh, the irony of the situation. It's simply bad luck, and I don't know what else to call it!

If I think about it, it was Aminata who besmirched my good name and landed me in a pitfall of disrespect — due to her carelessness. She was clearly not a professional. She always seemed to be preoccupied with something on her mind other than work.

She used to always act without thinking straight. At the salon, she used to daydream the whole time and ran into many accidents because of it. I bet she was thinking about Brian when she burned my client's hair.

I vividly remember that day. The poor lady shrieked at the top of her lungs, scaring the shit out of everyone, but Aminata was too lost to realize what had happened. Even the people passing by said that they could smell something burning.

It was the last nail in the coffin, and I had to fire her. All that, and here I was — helplessly at her mercy. Hiring her back to work at my salon was one of the biggest mistakes that I ever made. As I said, I only hired her because Brian caught me stealing supplies from that darned Pancake place.

He warned me that he would let the whole thing go if I did not hire his girl. As if she was not enough to bear, I also had to deal with him. He used to visit the salon every other day to ask for money. The worthless piece of rag that he was, I was sure that he did not work.

Hence, the visits after every few days to Aminata. It was apparent the guy could sell even his mother's kidney for some cash. He even dared to ask me for money once; imagine his girlfriend's employer! He should have been grateful that I gave his girlfriend a job despite her terrible salon skills.

That woman never earned any praise from any of her customers. In fact, people would even refuse to be served by her on their second visits. I would end up doing all the work that she should have done in the first place.

I don't think Brian realized that I was paying the amount his girlfriend used to lend him. Everything that Aminata did at work was messed up. She was the human-slave version of that elf in the famous movie.

***

"*Baby, I want an apology from her,*" Aminata said in her high-pitched, shrill voice, which was enough to give anyone a headache.

I swear, I have not heard a worse sound than her voice. She can scare the hell out of babies with her squeaky voice. She once told me that her former boyfriend loved her voice and called it sweet.

When she told me that, I thought: "I am confident he was lying, honey."

"*Don't worry, baby. She'll apologize all right,*" Brian replied with evident anger and revenge in his voice.

I tried to free myself, but he had me tied up pretty well. If only Vonn were this astute with our robbery planning. He is friendly, though.

"*Oh, my Vonn! Where are you? Find me before my ear starts bleeding because of Aminata's pinching voice.*" I thought to myself as I was lying helpless on the floor.

I kept my eyes closed so they didn't realize I was awake. The initial plan that I had was to free myself from the ropes and jump out of the vehicle when they slowed down the car on a speed breaker. It seems like a stretch now because they are not stopping anywhere.

I had been stuck in the backseat of their car for a while, and they had been constantly driving. I am not sure how kidnapping works, but shouldn't they have a place to move me to? I hoped they would so I could work on my plan B.

You see, I am the kind of person who always has a plan B ready — you know, just in case I need to make my way out of a situation. In this case, plan B was to act as if I was still knocked out while they moved me so that I could attempt to break free from them. My best shot at getting away from them was letting them think that I was unconscious.

I have successfully fooled many people since childhood. "*This shouldn't be too hard.*" I thought to myself.

After a few minutes, I accepted the fact that they were not going to stop anytime soon. I recalled that neither of them had a place, and they lived in their car. I feared that Brian had some other nasty plot brewing in his head. But I had to deal with that lunatic so often that I could smell his bullshit from a mile away.

Tired of laying in the back, I winced and made a faint noise as I had just woken up. I needed to know what they were up to. It jolted those two out of their trance.

"*Where am I?*" I said in a slurry and husky voice.

I was about to say, 'Who am I?' but I stopped myself halfway.

"*They shouldn't think I have lost my memory, or they will sedate me and sell my body parts for pennies.*" I thought to myself.

Brian reached out to the dashboard and picked a disgusting napkin to cover his face. It was hard to tell whether it was to be used for sanitary purposes or to clean this cursed four-wheeler that I was confined in. Aminata — being the dumb person she was — tried to copy her lover boy by searching her giant handbag for a napkin.

She could not find anything except a hair band with an artificial sunflower replica perched up in the center. The whole ordeal was pathetic. The two were bickering in their low-pitched voices. I repeated my performance once again to gather their attention.

It was fine this time around. Whoever said practice makes you perfect was not entirely wrong. Brian turned back and stated in a somewhat 'trying-to-scare-you-but-scared-myself voice':

"*I know what you are up to.*" He said in a miserable attempt to frighten me. I think they were also doing it for the first time. Kidnapping was clearly not their forte.

"*Mmmmm....*" I responded.

I acted like I could not understand him and had just gotten up from a long slumber.

"*I want a portion of that money you scored*," Brian said.

"*I see. That's what you're after.*" I thought to myself.

Brian was thinking to the full extent of his intellectual capacities and trying to get a big chunk. However, the fact that he spoke without noticing my response showed he did not care much about anything. It was evident he didn't have a plan in mind and just wanted to leave with the cash.

"*You better give us that or-*" Brian said.

He left the sentence midway for a dramatic effect. I'd rate his performance below average. Even a first-grader could have pulled this act better than him.

"*You must give us money or....*" Brian said.

He repeated the statement after realizing that his first attempt did not produce the desired response from my end.

"*And an apology as well!*" Aminata chipped in her painfully squeaky voice.

Just the sound of her voice boiled my blood.

"*Yeah. I will give you something for sure, minion. A slap, maybe for spoiling my reputation. But certainly not an apology.*" I thought to myself irritatedly.

"*Shut up, Am!*" Brian said harshly.

"*What?*" Aminata replied, seeming shocked at his response.

"*I am talking,*" Brian said with a sense of superiority in his voice.

"*I am also talking,*" Aminata poorly tried to make a point.

"*You should not,*" Brian said rather loudly as if to put her in her place.

"*Oh really? Who said so?*" Aminata snapped back.

They began to bicker among themselves once again, completely ignoring that I was in their backseat. I was shocked to see Aminata talk back to him. In the time she worked for me, she never had the nerve to disobey him, let alone talk back to him. Soon after, they stopped at a gas station to refill the tank.

I was sure the tank was empty since they had been driving it aimlessly for hours, maybe even before I hit their vehicle.

"*Go out and deal with the cash part,*" Brian commanded.

"*Let's take some from her,*" Aminata replied, shooting me a look filled with anger.

"*We can't do that right now,*" Brian replied.

"*Why not?*" Aminata was furious to hear this.

"*I scanned her while tying her up. She's clear.*" Brian said casually.

"*Well, I don't have money either,*" Aminata said, seeming stressed.

"*I am sure you do,*" Brian replied.

"*How can you say that?*" Aminata said, attempting to outsmart him.

"*Well. Didn't you fool that lady and get money out of her pocket?*" Brian said, referencing a recent incident.

Aminata was clearly shocked to hear it. It was apparent she didn't think he would know of that incident. The poor girl had no idea how cunning her boyfriend was.

"*I know you have the money, Am. So stop lying to my face and pay up!*" Brian ordered in his usual harsh tone.

Aminata believed what he said, being the obedient girlfriend she was. I have to say there was not much that had changed. I was hyping her up for no reason. I winced once more to gather their attention.

"*Please untie me.*" I tried to be loud this time.

I opened my eyes a little for a more impactful performance. Brian looked back and scanned me from head to toe. Ahaa! I knew this would work. It always does. My trump card is seduction. It always works.

"*Love...?*" I muttered.

Brian's eyes popped out with surprise. He could not believe that someone other than that blind Aminata could call him that.

"*Vonn?*" I added after a pause to clear things up.

After realizing that I was lost in my thoughts, using the term 'Love' to refer to someone else, Brian closed his mouth. There was something more to it — an opportunity that I couldn't let slip away.

"*Let me go*," I said in a husky voice filled with affection.

I'm sure that it was hard for him to focus solely on the money at this point. This was a tactic that I could effectively use to my advantage.

"*Hey. You. Let me go.*" I said once more as playfully as I could.

My voice was seductive and tempting. I knew that I had to use all the arrows in my quiver to get out of this situation, or else it could go very badly. They were fools, but they meant business, and I wasn't about to give up my hard-earned money for a couple of fools. I had to do something significant before Aminata returned.

"*Please, let's go somewhere and discuss,*" I added more to tease him.

It was a bold move, but I knew I had to provoke him enough to get a response.

"*What?*" He abruptly turned, looking confused.

His expressions were unfathomable — a combination of surprise, confusion, and curiosity. I knew what I did and said was unnerving for him. It was a reminder that I needed to add one more sentence to push him, and he'd come falling on his knees for me.

"*I am sure we can figure this out... together,*" I stated.

I could sense the air tensing and his expressions changing dramatically. I was entirely sure that it would be the moment when he would put the vehicle into gear and try to drive me somewhere else. He turned his head back toward the windshield; he was about to drive the car when Aminata opened the door to the passenger seat and settled herself back in.

"*Damn! It's unbelievable.*" Now, what do I do?

This fool has the worst timing; I almost had him!

Chapter 5: In Hope to Elope

"*Hey, you! I paid for it this time. Next time, it is your turn.*" Aminata said in her shrill and thin voice once she was in the car.

"*Oh, you think I am dumb? I saw you flirting with that brat.*" Brian retorted swiftly, his voice oozing with his characteristic abrasiveness.

"*Baby....*" Aminata opened her mouth to say something when Brian cut her short.

"*I know he did not ask for a penny from you. So, don't pull this 'you owe me' crap on me.*" Brian said to her.

In an instant, the car's atmosphere shifted dramatically. All my effort to escape had washed down the drain with Aminata being back in the car. The urge to surrender tugged at me, but I swiftly dismissed it. An internal voice resounded loudly, drowning out negativity.

"*You cannot give up. You are Mahogany!*" I thought to myself.

Maybe it was too early to call it quits. I mean, I did manage to lure Brian in with my charms within a few minutes. I was convinced the plan would have been set in motion if not for Aminata's ill-timed return. But why let a momentary setback dim my confidence?

Imagine what I could have done with more time! All I needed was a chance to be alone with Aminata's less-than-savory boyfriend so I could get out of there. Reassurance enveloped me as I mentally recounted my strengths, shoring up my wavering confidence. I revisited my past accomplishments mentally, rekindling my self-belief in my true capabilities.

I reminded myself of the art I had mastered—convincing people, bending their will until they came to the precipice of surrender.

"*I trust my skills. I got this.*" I told myself. The funny part is that most people are not good at playing people. But I am!

"*It is an art, and I am the artist,*" I told myself again.

A memory came back to me when someone had called out me for being "*persistent.*" His tone did not convey any admiration. In fact, it suggested persistence as an undesirable trait. Nevertheless, I appreciated the recognition, no matter the context.

Though many people perceived my persistence as a negative quality, I knew better. It was a trait not easily replicated. I acknowledged its value, and I understood that most people could never grasp its essence.

Over the years, I have mastered the art of drawing people in and making them begrudge the fact that they couldn't replicate my finesse. It's my strength, not a weakness—a power to wield, a weapon to deploy in the moments that counted. Anyway, I could take that kind of ignorance over what I had in front of me any day.

Those fools were engaged in an ongoing bickering match. Their discordant voices were grating on my ears. I swear to God, they were not meant to be humans. I hate that Brian was speaking because every time he opened his mouth, it felt like he was told to bark.

His voice was so displeasing that I felt like covering my ears. And if Brian was meant to be a rabid dog, Aminata was undoubtedly destined to be a bird. But not one of those lovely, melodious songbirds. No. She was the type of bird whose incessant twittering drills into your skull, giving birth to a pounding headache that takes up residence behind your eyes.

But enough of that distraction. What mattered now was regaining my sense of control and devising a plan to escape this situation. An urgency to reclaim my power surged within me, and I knew I had to find a way to break free as swiftly as possible.

***

Vonn's restlessness was palpable. An unyielding manifestation of the recent events had sent tremors through his world. The uncertainty surrounding Mahogany's whereabouts kept him on the edge — each passing second feeling like an eternity. His room, which was once a place of comfort, now felt confining as he paced back and forth — traversing the space like a caged lion. His mind echoed with his silent pleas — each one directed toward Mahogany's well-being.

"*Oh, Mahogany! Where are you?*" He thought.

While it seemed silly, I knew that he couldn't help but wish for the ability to connect with me telepathically — out of a desperate desire to know where I was so he could bring me back. In the midst of his agitated pacing, a new worry gnawed at his consciousness and halted him in his tracks. The weight of a potentially troubling conversation weighed heavily on his shoulders.

"*What would I say to her father?*" Vonn mumbled under his breath.

His eyebrows were furrowing in thought. The prospect of Mr. Worthy inquiring about his daughter's whereabouts loomed like an impending storm. The passing moments felt like an eternity when, finally, a resolution crystallized in Vonn's mind. He came up to the decision with a resolute expression on his face.

A mix of determination and worry fueled him. He left the room with a purposeful stride. The intent and his destination were evident in his mind now.

***

The ceaseless back-and-forth between Brian and Aminata was beginning to get on my nerves. Their constant need to one-up each other with reminders of favors exchanged felt like an endless loop of childish pettiness. The irritation that they provoked began to reach a boiling point.

I knew that I couldn't stay silent anymore. It was high time that I addressed their crap and, more importantly, found out their motives for this whole ordeal. However, just as I was about to break my silence and confront them, a subtle shift in Brian's driving caught my attention.

He made a sharp turn onto a residential street with an ease that suggested he was familiar with the area.

"*So, they did have a place?*" I thought to myself.

I felt optimistic, and hope began to bloom inside me. "*This could be my way out.*" I figured.

The prospect that they might have a designated place for whatever sinister plans they had in store sparked a surge of optimism. This newfound insight meant a potential opportunity for escape — a way for me to slip through their fingers. My determination soared, and my thoughts immediately turned towards adapting my plans to exploit this potential opening.

It was a fantastic idea — using their own designated hideout against them. With renewed purpose, I held my tongue and observed the surroundings. I was noting down every alleyway, turn, and signboard to memory. These details were vital pieces of a puzzle.

Suddenly, a map was etched into my mind that would ensure a smooth exit without any missteps. As the relentless bickering continued between Brian and Aminata, I remained quiet. My mind was solely focused on the task at hand.

"*Jesus! I am glad that they did not use a blindfold.*" I muttered under my breath, which thankfully went unnoticed in their non-stop squabbling.

After what felt like a considerable amount of time and a series of turns down progressively narrower streets, the vehicle finally came to a stop. I had already observed my surroundings. I had an aged and worn property in my sights.

The old property was a house that exuded an air of neglect. It was as if its owners had abandoned it years ago. The disheveled appearance of the bungalow indicated that it had fallen into disrepair over time.

"*Surely! They are illegally using the place.*" I thought to myself.

Given their financial circumstances, renting a property would likely be out of the question — let alone purchasing one. This revelation ignited a spark of hope within me. If they were relatively new to this location, their familiarity with the house might be limited. This meant I could exploit their lack of knowledge and find a way to break free from their captivity.

I only needed to know for how long they had been using this place. If they had taken hold of it relatively recently, it was a sign that they did not know the place inside out. It meant that there were more chances to trap my captors and use their lack of knowledge to run away from their confining shackles.

My mind raced as it formulated a plan in an instant. All I needed was to convince one of them to release me temporarily — allowing me to move about the premises. By navigating the house, I could gather essential information, scout potential escape routes, and identify vulnerabilities to exploit. The key was to employ strategy over brute force.

"*Force does not always work; the strategy does.*" One of my favorite salon customers had once told me, and so I gladly embraced this quote.

I was resolute in my approach. It was evident that tactics and finesse would be my allies in this predicament. I needed a plan that conserved my energy, saving it for the crucial moments to escape. Scaling walls and making a run for it required physical strength, which was a resource I couldn't afford to squander prematurely.

With determination, I made a mental pact with myself that I was committed to escaping this situation unscathed. By doing so, I would be preserving my strength for the pivotal moments ahead. This self-assurance and self-belief was my anchor — a steadfast reminder of my goal to break free.

"*I need to divert my focus to Aminata as she was the weaker link in this duo.*" I thought to myself.

She was clearly dumber than Brian, which made her the perfect candidate for manipulation. My plan began to take shape as I thought that intoxicating Brian would be the best way to minimize any potential physical altercations. If things went south, then I would get Aminata to set me free through careful manipulation.

As I strategized, the vehicle jolted to a rough stop, and this signaled our arrival. Aminata exited the car, followed by Brian, and they began to get ready to transfer me into the house. Maybe I needed to divert my energies toward Aminata first since she was dumb, which meant that she was a better option to begin with.

So, I just needed to intoxicate Brian. This would ensure that there was less struggle if things came down to being physical. While I was making plans and keeping all the options open, Brian parked the car roughly on the side. Aminata exited the car and joined her boyfriend to transfer me inside the house.

I remained passive, choosing not to put up a struggle as I had initially considered upon waking up in their vehicle. Instead, I opted to bide idle and wait for the right moment. Being patient was akin to nurturing a seed and waiting for it to blossom into a tree of opportunity.

Thus, I followed their lead without resistance. Aminata led the way down a corridor and halted in front of a spacious room resembling a television lounge. While Brian stayed behind to lock the door, I refrained from engaging in any physical confrontation with Aminata. The fruit was hanging low as I was waiting for the right opportunity.

Hence, I stayed quiet while they led me in. Aminata crossed a corridor and finally stopped in front of a large room resembling a T.V. lounge. At this moment, Brian was in the back to lock the door. I could have done a one-to-one combat with that skinny Aminata at that time.

She could not definitely fight me back all on her own. But, I realized that my lack of knowledge about the property could jeopardize my escape. Fleeing recklessly might result in my captors securing the premises, foiling any of my future attempts at escape.

My determination to succeed was unwavering, but I understood that a strategic approach was necessary to hatch a successful escape plan.

"*Divide and conquer.*" I reminded myself of my plan.

"*You don't deserve such disrespect,*" I said empathetically to Aminata.

Unexpectedly, breaking my silence caught her off guard.

"*Shut up, you bitch*!" Aminata replied with a nasty expression, showing the hatred that she harbored for me.

Brian joined us moments later, becoming the cue for me to initiate my plan. Engaging them in conversation, I bombarded them with questions, aiming to glean information about their familiarity with the area and the house.

This was the moment I began to execute my plans. I started talking non-stop in front of them. I was throwing questions at them in an attempt to take out some information.

"*So, you two seem pretty familiar with this place. How long have you been squatting here?*"

Aminata looked at me with an irritated glance, but I could see through Brian's eyes that he was suspicious.

"*Why do you care, huh?*" Brian snapped, with his usual aggression present in his voice.

I shrugged as much as my restraints allowed. "*Just curious, considering you seem so comfortable.*"

Aminata crossed her arms defensively. "*We've been around long enough. Don't think it's any of your business.*"

I pressed on, my tone casual yet probing. "*Must be nice to know the ins and outs of the place. You know, just in case.*"

Brian's eyebrow furrowed, and his guard was clearly up. "*What are you implying?*"

I tilted my head slightly, feigning innocence. "*Oh, nothing. It's just interesting how you managed to find this spot so easily.*"

Aminata exchanged a glance with Brian before answering: "*We have our ways.*"

Leaning back as far as my restraints allowed, I fixed my gaze on Brian.

"*Speaking of ways, you both seemed pretty confident about my little venture. How'd you know about it?*"

Brian's expression didn't change, but I noticed a flicker of unease in his eyes. "*We hear things, Mahogany.*"

Brian told me they knew about my robbery plan and wanted their fair share. I decided to push a bit harder. "*Did you hear enough to know the specifics? Like the location, timing, everything?*"

Aminata shifted uncomfortably. "*Enough to know you had some scheme going on.*"

I chuckled with a hint of disbelief in my voice. "*Impressive. Must be some well-connected grapevine that you're tapping into.*"

"*Fair share? Were they serious? Who am I? Their mother? Who shall inherit them a part of whatever she owns?*" I was fuming inside when I thought about this, but I chose to keep it all to myself.

Brian's jaw clenched, but his tone remained guarded. " *We know more than you think.*"

I decided to steer the conversation in a different direction. "*So, you're looking for a 'fair share'? How much are we talking about here?*"

Aminata rolled her eyes, clearly frustrated with my line of questioning. "*Enough to make up for the trouble you caused.*"

I leaned forward slightly, a mockingly innocent smile on my lips. "*But what's 'fair'? I mean, you didn't exactly earn it, did you?*"

Brian's patience was wearing thin. "*Enough games, Mahogany*!" Aminata added she wanted an apology as well.

I came up with a situation at that exact moment. I told them that the money was trapped and they needed to do something to get it first.

I tilted my head, studying them both. "*And what if I were to help you retrieve that money?*"

Brian's expression hardened, his suspicion growing. " *Why would you do that?*"

I shrugged, a sly grin tugging at my lips. "*Call it insurance. Maybe we can work together and ensure everyone gets what they want.*"

The tension in the room was almost tangible. I could see them considering my proposal; their expressions were mixed with uncertainty and greed. It was a delicate balance, but I had successfully planted the seeds of doubt in their minds.

"*Ask your damn daddy to bring it to us!*" Brian replied in an outburst, his words dripping with skepticism.

I realized at that moment that these guys would not let me go without getting paid for their struggle. My bad fate brought me to this duo, but now only my wisdom can save me from this trouble. My mind raced, considering my next move.

I had to buy time, exhaust their energies, and find an opportunity to slip away.

"*I wish I could,*" I replied, feigning defeat.

"*But you know how it is with family. They're not always willing to bail you out of every situation.*" I continued.

Brian rolled his eyes, clearly unimpressed. I could see the weariness etched on his face from the hours on the road and the constant bickering. I continued my blabbering, taking the reins of the conversation to wear them down further.

As Aminata's eyes drooped, I seized the chance. I knew I had to act swiftly before they realized my plan.

"*Hey, Aminata.*" I said with a slightly mischievous grin, "*I really need to use the washroom. Like, urgently. If you don't take me now, I'll have to relieve myself right here.*"

Aminata's eyes widened in alarm, and she quickly complied. The seemingly mundane and abrupt request gave me a golden opportunity to analyze the layout of the house and locate a possible escape route — a broken window.

"*Small opportunities lead to big victories*," I told myself.

Hours passed, and exhaustion began to overtake them. Brian fell into a deep sleep and instructed Aminata to keep watch. I kept myself awake, determined to execute the plan. As Aminata's fatigue caught up with her, I carefully used a sharp tool I found to free myself from the ropes.

Moving silently, I reached the window I had marked earlier, and I found that it was shattered. Perhaps there was a previous escape attempt, but I carefully squeezed my way through the broken glass as I did not want to cut myself into the scattered fragments.

I had to be swift and cautious since my sneakers were serving as my silent companions in this stealthy endeavor. Once outside, my heart raced as I sprinted toward the road. Each step was driven by the adrenaline coursing through my veins.

The thought of reaching safety consumed my mind, and I was thinking of Vonn to come to my rescue. I was constantly reassuring myself about the possibility of my success in an attempt to boost my confidence. With each stride, I repeated my favorite mantras:

"*I can do this*!" and "*Keep going.*"

I was running as fast as possible to make it to a place from where I could call Vonn to come to my rescue. And then, just as the exhilaration of my escape began to wash over me, a voice pierced the silence.

"*Hey, you!*" The shout echoed around me, making me skip a heartbeat.

"*But did I escape, really? Who is that?*" I asked myself.

Chapter 6: Judgment Day

(Part 1)

As I sprinted through the dimly lit streets, my breath came back as I was enraged and running fast. The weight of my bookbag, carrying the precious money that could be my ticket to freedom, thudded against my back with every step. Panic and determination fueled my every move.

I had to keep going and escape the clutches of Brian and Aminata before they caught up to me. My heart raced in tandem with my footsteps. The sound of my breathing was loud enough for my ears.

With each turn I took, I hoped I was putting more distance between myself and my captors. It was then that I saw a figure up ahead — standing under a flickering streetlight. My mind registered the person as a man, and a voice inside me screamed for caution. But I was running on pure instinct now, and my legs carried me closer to him before I could think twice.

"*Hey! Who's there?*" the man called me out in a Jamaican accent. His voice cut through the darkness, sending jolts down my spine.

"*Oh, what the hell now! Why can't I get home in peace?*" " I thought to myself.

"*Hey! Are you all right?*" There was genuine concern that laced his voice as he was offering me a glimmer of hope that I wasn't alone in this desperate situation.

I skidded to a stop before him as I wanted to catch a breath and let my body relax for a bit. For a brief moment, I considered just running past him because I did not know if I could trust him. There was just something in his eyes, perhaps a mixture of compassion and recognition, that made me hesitate and stop.

"*Please, you've got to help me.*" I gasped as my voice was barely above a whisper as I fought to catch my breath. "*They're after me.*"

His eyebrows furrowed in genuine concern, and he spoke to me: "*Hold on, don't worry. Just tell me what happened.*"

As I opened my mouth to respond, the words caught in my throat. The man's features became clearer under the dim light, and a wave of realization crashed over me. It was him. The memory weighed heavily on my conscience, a memory I had tried to bury deep within me, but I was now faced with the consequences of my actions.

All this just resurfaced with a haunting clarity. I couldn't believe it was him. I couldn't believe it was all happening to me. It felt like the day of judgment was upon me, and my hell was an endless loop of running into people I had wronged throughout my life.

So, to backtrack a bit and tell who he was, we were in a relationship, and it had begun innocently enough. Eventually, we went through a whirlwind of laughter, shared secrets, and stolen moments. But as time went on, I began to feel trapped by the expectations that came with commitment.

So, I made a series of ill-conceived decisions. I started distancing myself from Jayden, ignoring his calls and messages. I avoided him whenever I could, making feeble excuses and promises I had no intention of keeping. I knew it was cowardly to end things, but in my mind, it seemed easier than facing the truth.

As if my callous actions weren't enough, I took it a step further. One evening, at a community gathering, I overheard rumors about Jayden's professional aspirations and how they were crushed when we were involved. The rumors remarked how well he had done for himself ever since he moved on from me and how I was everything wrong with him.

Instead of addressing the issue maturely, I let my pride and insecurity get the best of me. In a moment of recklessness, I decided to spread false rumors, insinuating that Jayden had used unethical means to advance his career. The words left my lips without a second thought, fueled by a mix of jealousy and a desire to protect my image.

I never stopped to consider the consequences of my actions and the lives I could potentially ruin. The aftermath was catastrophic. The rumors spread like wildfire, tarnishing Jayden's reputation and causing a chain reaction within the community.

Colleagues, ostracized by friends, shunned him and eventually blackballed him from the very opportunities he had worked so hard to secure. Worse yet, the woman he had planned to marry, his fiancée, saw him in a new light— one tainted by doubt and mistrust.

She couldn't ignore the whispers and innuendos, and the foundation of their relationship crumbled beneath the weight of my deceit. The weight of my guilt bore down on me; each look at him was a painful reminder of the damage that I had inflicted him with.

Jayden's voice echoed in my mind — a haunting refrain of hurt and betrayal. It was a wound I had caused him, and now, fate circled back to have us cross paths once again. My mind raced as I tried to come up with an explanation, as I was trying to find a way to avoid the inevitable confrontation.

Maybe he wouldn't recognize me in the darkness, I thought desperately, but my hopes were dashed as he continued speaking.

"*Miss? Who's after you? What do you need me?*" Jayden's voice held a hint of frustration now as his eyebrows furrowed, and he took a step closer.

"*I...*" I stammered as my mind raced to find a way out. But before I could form a coherent sentence, Jayden's expression changed from concern to recognition. His eyes widened as if a sudden realization had hit him like a ton of bricks.

"*It's you!*" His voice revealed a precise mixture of disbelief and anger.

Before he could finish his sentence, my heart sank. There was no escaping it now — he knew who I was, and he knew what I had done. The guilt and shame washed over me — threatening to overwhelm my already-frayed nerves.

"*I know I messed up.*" I finally managed to blurt out, my voice barely above a whisper. "*I know I hurt you, and I'm so, so sorry.*"

Jayden's anger did not soften at my words. It was clear that forgiveness wouldn't come quickly. He crossed his arms, as his expressions were a mix of frustration and anger.

"*I lost everything because of you,*" he said quietly. His voice was burdened with emotions. "*My reputation, my dreams, even the woman I was going to marry... all gone because of your lies, Mahogony.*"

Tears pricked at the corners of my eyes as the weight of my actions crashed down on me once again. I had ruined his life, shattered his dreams, and caused pain beyond measure.

"*I know I can never make it right, Jayden,*" I said, as I felt a genuine contempt and disdain for my actions and words.

My voice was shaking with remorse. "*But please, Jayden, I need your help. I need a ride to town. I was kidnapped, and they tied me up. I don't know what they were going to do with me. I've been gone for days, and my family must be worried sick.*"

"*Well, most of it is true. They did kidnap me, and they were crazy enough to do whatever they wanted.*" I thought to myself.

"*A little white lie won't hurt him, and besides, it's the only way I'll get out of here. Brian and Aminata would catch me real quick if I tried to make my way back home on foot.*" I talked to myself.

Jayden hesitated as his eyes locked with mine for a long and tense moment. It felt like an eternity before he finally let out a heavy sigh and nodded.

"*Get in.*" His voice was weary as he gestured toward his car.

We sat in silence. For a while, the only sound was the soft hum of the engine and the distant echo of my racing thoughts. There was an awkward silence between the two of us as we were thinking.

"*Why should I help you?*" Jayden's voice broke the silence as his eyes were still fixed on the road ahead.

"*I could just leave you here to rot. That's what I should do, considering what you did to me.*"

I took a deep breath, trying to find the right words to convey the depth of my regret and desperation. "*I messed up, Jayden, and I'm paying for it now. But-*"

"*Who do you think you are, Mahogony?*" Jayden interrupted my sentence. His voice was dripping with anger, but his eyes were laser-focused on the road. He continued:

"*Do you have any idea about the pain that you inflict upon people? You ruined me, and for what? To soothe your ego and feed your pride? Do you have any empathy for anybody other than yourself? Do you think people will keep taking your shit and rescuing you from the messes that you keep getting yourself into, in spite of how you treat them? I should dump your ass here and let you rot in the consequences of your actions. You must've done something to get where you are. I'm sure of it.*"

Jayden's words crashed into me like a tidal wave, each one hitting harder than the last. The pain in his voice cut through my heart, exposing the truth that I had spent so long trying to ignore. I had hurt him, hurt him deeply, and I was facing the consequences of my actions now.

Tears welled up in my eyes as his anger washed over me. I felt small and insignificant — like a child feels after being scolded for a grave mistake. He was right, of course. I had acted recklessly, thoughtlessly, and without ever considering the impact of my actions on others.

"*I'm so sorry,*" I choked out, my voice cracked with emotions. "*I never meant for any of this to happen. I didn't think about the consequences. I didn't think about you.*"

Jayden's grip on the steering wheel remained tight. His jaw clenched in frustration. "*You think a simple 'I'm sorry' can undo what you've done? You think it can bring back what I've lost?*"

"*No,*" I whispered, as tears were streaming freely down my cheeks. "*I don't expect you to forgive me, Jayden. I don't deserve your forgiveness. But I want to change. I want to make things right. And if you let me, I want to start by helping you, by helping you get back on your feet.*"

Jayden's grip on the steering wheel tightened, his knuckles turning white. "*You think you can just waltz back into my life and fix everything?*" he said with a tinged bitterness in his voice.

"*No,*" I replied softly as my gaze fixed on my hands in my lap. "*But I want to try. I want to make amends to prove that I've changed. If you get me to town, I'll owe you.*"

His eyes were set on mine, and in the dim light, I could see a storm of emotions swirling within his eyes.

"*You don't owe me anything.*" He replied curtly, his tone laced with a bitterness that I couldn't ignore.

I felt a lump forming in my throat as I struggled to find the right words. "*I know I messed up, and I'm truly sorry for everything I put you through.*"

(Part 2)

"*You're messed up big time!*" He said with his expressions stone cold and his gaze laser-focused on the car.

"*Boy, it's going to be a long ride.*" I thought to myself.

***

Vonn and Nicole were diligently tending to the customers back at the salon. The atmosphere was lively and filled with the usual chatter and laughter that accompanied a busy salon. Nicole, as usual, had the 6 p.m. news playing on a small TV in the corner. She liked to stay updated on current events, even while working.

Today, however, her attention was drawn to the screen more intently than usual. On the TV, DJ Element was sitting beside a nosy reporter, giving details about the recent robbery. He appeared flustered and agitated, running his hand through his slick hair as he spoke.

"*I don't remember much, but there was a man and a woman. They stole thousands of dollars from me. Thousands! This is ridiculous! I need to get those bastards. Anyone who gives me a worthy tip about their whereabouts will get a $10,000 reward!*"

Nicole couldn't believe her eyes. "*Oh shit! We have got to get in touch with Mahogany.*" She muttered under her breath and then called out to Vonn — waving at him. Vonn, who was in the middle of cutting a customer's hair, froze in his tracks.

His heart raced, and his hands shook as he glanced at the TV. The nervousness got the best of him, and as he resumed snipping, he accidentally chopped a square chunk off the customer's curly hair. The customer let out an unexpected yelp.

Vonn's eyes widened, and he quickly assessed the damage. Flustered, he pointed to the back office, signaling the customer to follow him. Nicole gathered a notepad and briskly walked behind him.

She said to Maurice, another stylist: "*Keep an eye on the shop; we're working on inventory.*"

As they walked back to the storage room, Vonn turned to the customer whose hair he had botched and said, "*I'm so sorry, sir. The cut's on the house today. And you can pick any hat or toupee you want from the store.*"

The older gentleman, still agitated with a makeshift bald spot, raised a disapproving eyebrow but eventually gave in. He grabbed both the free haircut and a snazzy toupee and gave Vonn the middle finger on his way out.

Nicole couldn't contain her laughter. "*Man, you got Elder Smith hot. You know Mahogany will never let you live that one down.*"

Vonn sighed and ran a hand through his hair, trying to regain his composure. "*I thought this shit with Element had cooled down. Now he's on TV with that nosey Ella Chapman, acting like a badass. The CAM 5 news had to bleep out half of what he said.*"

The two of them exchanged a worried glance. The salon had enough drama to deal with, but DJ

Element's reappearance on the news was a whole new level of trouble. Nicole took a deep breath.

"*Where are you, Mahogany? Shit's getting crazy up here.*" She thought to herself. Her eyes still darted between the TV screen and her surroundings.

The news of the robbery and DJ Element's accusations had shaken her.

"*We got our owner missing. We don't need no more problems to happen,*" she muttered as her voice was filled with worry.

Vonn and Nicole exchanged another uneasy glance. Then, taking a deep breath, they both composed themselves.

"*Vonn, listen to me carefully.*" Nicole turned to Vonn: "*Mahogany is on her way back, and that's our daily until it happens.*"

Vonn nodded in agreement, as his hands were still slightly trembling from the shock of the news report. He had already given up on me, as he was assuming I had run off with the bounty. After all, it would not be the first time that she did that.

Hopefully, 'Big Dick' Wallace wasn't part of the plan. But now, with the news of the robbery and DJ Element's accusations, it seemed like a whole new storm was brewing. Nicole thought for a moment and then made a decision.

She reached for her phone and dialed my number, hoping that I would pick up. Vonn watched her; his expression was a mixture of doubt and hope. The phone rang, and they both held their breath — waiting for a response from their friend.

After a few anxious seconds, a voice finally spoke through the other end. "*Hello?*"

"*Mahogany, it's Nicole!*" she said, as relief washed over her as she heard my voice. "*Fool, you've been gone for several days,*" Nicole spoke with annoyance and amusement.

"*I have been through hell, and I escaped, and now I have a ride back from Jayden,*" I explained quickly, eager to share the news.

"*Girl...*" I could hear Nicole chuckling from the other end. "*I could have sworn you said you got a ride back to Alexandria from Jayden.*"

My response left Nicole momentarily stunned. "*That's correct. I do.*"

Vonn, who had been listening to the conversation, couldn't hold back his frustration any longer. "*That slick, bow-legged, lying SOB!*"

"*Calm down, Vonn. We are not friendly.*" I said firmly. "*He saved my life. See you in an hour.*" And with that, she cut the call.

Nicole and Vonn exchanged skeptical glances. The situation had just taken another unexpected turn, leaving them both wondering what kind of trouble I had gotten myself into this time.

Chapter 7: Mahogany's Return

I was about to return soon, but till then, Vonn and Nicole had to cover for me in whichever way they could, from the police and my clients, the most demanding of which was a woman named Lady Colbert. Lady Colbert, much to the dread of Nicole and Vonn, entered the salon with an air of overenthusiasm. Vonn and Nicole exchanged glances, sensing trouble.

Vonn raised an eyebrow and looked at Nicole, "*What the hell? Lady Colbert? Like we didn't have enough on our plates already! You deal with her; I've got my hands full here.*"

"*Only Mahogany has the patience to deal with her,*" replied Nicole, visibly irritated. "*God, where is she anyway?*"

"*I need a cut and color, and I need it now!*" Lady Colbert insisted, oblivious to the tension in the room.

Lady Colbert was the kind of woman to talk one's ear off if given the chance. She was in her fifties and had been coming to my salon for years. She would insist on recounting her escapades to me every time. Since I wasn't there, Nicole had to bear the brunt.

"*Be right there, Lady Colbert!*" Nicole shouted.

Whispering to Vonn, she said, " *Vonn, I'm going to need a cut of that money. I swear my stress levels are through the roof dealing with Mahogany's mess.*"

Vonn smirked, "*You think you're the only one stressed? This is a team effort.*"

Lady Colbert interrupted, *"Where's Mahogany? I've got some juicy gossip for her!"*

Nicole hesitated, then sighed, "*Mahogany's not here. She's... on a break. But I can take care of your hair, no problem. Only a root touchup, right?*"

"*Ugh! That girl...*" Lady Colbert said, agitated as she looked around the room.

" *Well, I guess business is slow here. All right, sweet cheeks, guess it's your lucky day.*" As Lady Colbert settled into the chair, Nicole muttered to Vonn: " *This is a disaster waiting to happen.*"

Vonn nodded, "*Tell me about it. We're running a salon and a cover-up operation at the same time.*"

Lady Colbert sat in the plush black and white chair. Nicole, with a sly smile, began working on Lady Colbert's hair. " *You know, Lady C, Mahogany talks so much about you; from what I hear, you're her favorite client. Know why?*"

" *Why?*" asked Lady Colbert.

"*Because your chats make her day.*" Nicole smiled.

"*Well, then, you better strap in!*" Lady Colbert was all set to entertain Nicole and Vonn with her incessant rants and further churn the rumor mill.

Seated comfortably in Nicole's chair, she began the conversation in a casual tone: "*You won't believe what's happening in town. The mall sales are through the roof, and there's a scandal at the massage parlor.*"

Vonn, stifling his laugh, couldn't resist letting out a snicker. "*What kind of scandal are we talking about here?*"

Nicole, concentrating on Lady Colbert's hair, listened intently as she created horizontal rows in the lower sections and vertical rows in the top.

Lady Colbert continued, "*Apparently, the massage parlor got busted for providing happy endings to over a thousand men and two hundred women in Northern Virginia.*"

Vonn raised an eyebrow, trying to stifle another chuckle. "*Well, that's quite the customer satisfaction guarantee.*"

Lady Colbert continued, "*Also! Do you know Deacon Titus? Well, he was one of them. When he got busted, guess what he did? He came to the front of the church and...*"

Lady Colbert continued with a hint of mischief in her voice. "*He asked for forgiveness! His wife was so embarrassed. He claimed he hadn't had any action since the George W. days. You know, post-presidential drought.*" Lady Colbert shared, her eyes twinkling with amusement.

Vonn burst into laughter, unable to contain himself, and couldn't resist a witty comment. "*Well, what's a man supposed to do? It's been a long, dry spell for him.*"

Amidst the banter, Vonn turned the spotlight on Nicole. "*Those folks on Fullerton Ave are a different breed, huh? Pervs, I tell you. Hey, Nicole, doesn't your momma live over there, too, on Fullerton Ave?*"

Nicole, with a playful yet firm demeanor, swung a wooden brush in Vonn's direction, smacking his shoulder. "*Watch it, Vonn. Your humor is getting us into enough trouble as it is.*"

Slightly embarrassed, she added, "*And thanks to the neighborhood gossip, I can't escape it even at work.*"

As more customers entered the salon, the lively conversation continued, blending humor, scandal, and neighborhood gossip. As Nicole skillfully sectioned Lady Colbert's hair, the salon began to fill with more customers. Vonn greeted them while keeping an eye on Nicole's subtle signals. Nicole, in between her stylist duties, caught snippets of conversations around the salon.

"*Oh, and did you hear that my husband got a DUI?*" Lady Colbert continued.

Vonn, still recovering from the wooden brush hit, chimed in, "*No, but I think we're in too deep already. Might as well hear the rest.*"

As Nicole worked on Lady Colbert's hair, the juicy gossip continued to flow. Lady Colbert spilled about not only the massage parlor scandal but also delved into details about her husband's DUI incident and her involvement in creating outfits for a luxurious event on the Potomac.

Meanwhile, the other customers couldn't help but eavesdrop on Lady Colbert's revelations. The salon buzzed with excitement and curiosity. Nicole seized the opportunity to promote the salon's services, trying to milk Lady Colbert for the money she was worth.

"*By the way,*" Nicole interjected, "*If you're preparing for that ritzy event, don't forget about the essentials – a wax and a fabulous manicure. We've got you covered.*"

Toya, a young woman overhearing their conversation, laughed, "*Oh, I've got the outfit for that down to the last detail; it's an ivory-colored masterpiece, which I'll pair with gold stilettos.*"

She gestured to the older lady, her sister, who had looked more like her mother, who then joined the conversation: "*I'll be clutching my pearls. The ID and event ticket? Right here in my bosom. No need for extras when I'll be on the ballroom floor all night.*"

Lady Colbert, not one to be left out, chimed in: "*Oh, you won't believe the creations I've been working on for that event. Dresses, suits, you name it. I've got two assistants helping me day and night.*"

The other patrons exchanged impressed glances. Lady Colbert's status as the district attorney's wife explained her involvement in such a prestigious affair. As the salon continued to bustle with activity, Nicole and Vonn navigated the delicate balance of hairdressing and covert conversations. The air was filled with the scent of hair dye, the hum of hairdryers, and the lively banter of a salon that doubled as a hub for both style and secrets.

***

Meanwhile, I navigated the streets in Jayden's car, constantly looking over my shoulder, unaware of the chaos unfolding back at the salon. When we reached, I practically leaped out of Jayden's car and gave him a hurried thanks, barely audible over the revving engine.

"*Thanks, Jayden. And...sorry!*" I called out as Jayden sped off.

"*Screw yourself, Mahogany,*" Jayden shouted back at me from the driver's seat, screeching his tires as he sped off.

In my typical fashion, I dialed Vonn's number. "*Come outside, Vonn. I'm back!*" I exclaimed, my voice carrying a sense of urgency and impatience.

Vonn's voice came through the phone, slightly muffled by the salon's background noise. "*Mahogany? I'm busy with a customer. Lady Colbert is in here. Just wait in the back.*" he instructed before quickly ending the call.

I let out a sigh, born of frustration, "*Well, damn!*" I muttered as I paced slightly on the sidewalk.

Needing a moment to collect myself, I took a deep breath. With a decisive exhale, I then strolled to the back of the salon, where Vonn had told me to wait. All the while, I had been carrying the weight of the bookbag filled with cash, which I needed to store somewhere ASAP.

"*Goddamn...where do I put this thing?*". I said, puzzled, looking around the room, when suddenly my gaze landed on a trunk.

I swiftly placed the bag in the trunk, closing it with a sense of relief, waiting for Nicole and Vonn to come. I began to settle in and overheard Lady Colbert continuing her saga of gossip to a captive audience of salon customers. Yearning to relax for a bit, I decided to freshen up.

A quick shower washed away the tensions of the day, and then I put on an oversized company t-shirt. Digging through Nicole's exercise bag, I found a pair of biker shorts and clean underwear —making myself comfortable in my dear friend's belongings. Now, there was another problem: I was starving.

Overcome with hunger, my eyes now fell on Nicole's footlong sandwich that she had packed. Succumbing to temptation, I indulged in a heavy sandwich all by myself on the couch. Exhausted from my escapades, I thought to settle in for a nap, with the soft hum of the salon murmurs serving as white noise.

As I drifted into a brief slumber, the weight of the day began to fade. The salon, a hub for both creativity and covert activities, held its secrets as I found a moment of peace on a rather hectic day.

***

As the last customer left, Vonn and Nicole seamlessly transitioned into cleanup mode. They swept and mopped the place, as was the usual routine.

Vonn, glancing around, remarked, "*Another day, another dollar, right, Nic?*"

Nicole, wiping down salon chairs, nodded. "*And another set of secrets spilled. Lady Colbert practically turned this place into a confessional today.*"

Vonn chuckled, "*Salons are like therapy sessions with better hairstyles. Speaking of which, Mahogany is in the back.*"

Nicole focused on sanitizing equipment and yelled, "*What? She's here?*"

"*She didn't call you? I told her to wait while we clean up,*" replied Vonn. "*I should check on her, though. Will you finish up?*"

"*I've already done more than my pay grade today; what's one thing more? Go!*" Nicole ordered him.

Vonn set aside his cleaning equipment and headed towards the back, where he stumbled upon a peacefully resting Mahogany curled up on the couch. While Vonn checked on Mahogany, Nicole meticulously continued her cleaning spree and tackled the bathroom and breakroom. She was wiping down all salon equipment: salon chairs, salon stations, wash area chairs, the receptionist desk, and the waiting room furniture and processing area equipment.

When Vonn returned, Nicole was scrubbing away in the breakroom. "*She's in dreamland. And you know what that means – more beauty sleep.*"

Nicole smirked, "*Maybe we should join her. After we finish here, of course.*"

And so, Vonn and Nicole put the finishing touches on the salon, which was now pristine and closed for the day.

After lockup, Vonn burst into the back of the salon, excitement written all over his face, and jolted her awake. "*Mahogany! You're a sight for sore eyes!*"

***

Now, I was wide awake from the jump and replied, "*Vonn! Goddamn it, I was sleeping like a baby!*"

I returned the hug, but as Vonn lingered for a passionate kiss, I playfully pushed him away. "*Keep it in your pants, Vonn. We've got business to discuss!*"

Vonn grinned, "*Business can wait for a moment.*" He leaned in and planted a long, lingering kiss on me as we briefly moaned. "*There, now we can talk.*"

I rolled her eyes but couldn't hide the smile on my face. "*Did you count your half of the money?*"

Vonn nodded, his grin widening. "*Yep, a clean 25,000. Not bad for a day's work, huh?*"

I smirked at him, "*Not bad at all. I've got some jewelry, too. About 15,000 worth.*"

Vonn raised an eyebrow, intrigued. "*Jewelry, huh? Nice touch. We make quite the team.*"

As we discussed our gains, I decided to address the situation with Nicole, first checking if she wasn't nearby to hear us talk.

"*By the way, Vonn, Nicole knows about... our little operation. If there are any earrings in that stash, give them to her for hush money. Otherwise, you'll be hearing her asking for more every time.*"

Vonn's expression shifted to contemplation, "*Nicole knows? Well, that complicates things.*"

I nodded, "*But she's willing to help, considering this isn't her main gig. If you want to keep her silent, share the spoils.*"

Vonn chuckled, "*Earrings it is, then.*"

I grinned: "*And who knows, she might become a permanent fixture in our little enterprise. A partner in crime, so to speak.*"

Vonn's eyes gleamed with amusement: "*Nicole, a partner in crime? That's a wild card I didn't see coming.*"

My concern lingered as I assessed our options for selling the jewelry. "*So, do you know anybody who can take these jewels off our hands?*"

Vonn, responding quickly, grinned, "*Good old King.*"

My eyes widened upon hearing those words, "*Hell no! That's my sister's ex.*"

Vonn, playfully but firmly, stomped his foot. "*Oh, come on. You know as well as I do that Wallace is the guy.*"

I shot him a skeptical look, "*Don't even think about it. He's known for ripping people off.*"

"*Okay, okay,*" I conceded, "*let's ask Nicole. She's the voice of reason with that crooked wig on.*" We both then shared a laugh at Nicole's expense.

All of a sudden, amid our planning, Nicole stormed into the room, clearly not in the best mood after her intense cleaning spree.

"*Vonn!*" shouted Nicole. "*You have the bathrooms tomorrow; I'm telling you right now. Well, well, if it isn't Mahogany in the flesh. So, are you finally going to tell us about your kidnapping?*"

"*I'll take a rain check on that,*" I replied, "*I was just asking Vonn who the best jeweler in town is.*"

Nicole replied curtly, "*Nobody here! I'd say go to Brooklyn. Do the bidding there and come back with a boatload of cash.*"

Nicole then handed Vonn a card with the name Pastor Epps slapped across it. "*Here, go see Pastor Epps. He'll take care of you.*"

Vonn glanced at the card, recognizing the name. "*This calls for a road trip,*" Vonn said. "*Pastor Epps, eh? The man who turns our shady deals into gold.*"

I smirked, "*Or at least into cash we can spend. Nicole, you're a lifesaver.*"

Nicole, still irritated, brushed off the compliment:

"*Just get it done, and don't mess it up. I don't want any more drama around here. And Mahogany, next time you decide to get kidnapped, give us a heads up. It messes with the salon schedule.*"

I couldn't help but chuckle. "*Yeah, yeah, message received. No more kidnapping without a prior warning. Now, let's hit the road.*"

Chapter 8: Brooklyn

Vonn and I cruised down the highway all the way to Brooklyn on a mission to meet the notorious Pastor Epps. Nicole decided to stay back since there had to be someone who could look after the salon. Pastor Epps had a particular reputation attached to his name; rumor has it that he used to be a master thief and an extortionist. Currently, he was the proud owner of a pawn shop owner; go figure.

"*So, how come this Pastor guy owns a whole shop after leaving his life behind as a conman?*" I asked Vonn. My attention was on the steering wheel, yet I still managed to munch on the snacks we had gotten for the road trip.

"*Maybe it's just a remix to his life soundtrack – swapping crime beats for cash notes,*" Vonn replied, trying to eat his fill before I could finish everything.

All we needed to do was exchange the stolen jewelry for some cold, hard cash. And who better to help with that than Pastor Epps – the man and the legend himself?

The anticipation in the car was tangible; I steered the ship, determined as ever, "*So, why not run a legit pawn shop, right? Turn that sketchy past into a money-making present.*"

Vonn, his fingers tapping out a rhythm on the dashboard, throws in his two cents. "*Exactly! It's like a new hustle, but with less risk and more pawned treasures.*"

As we hit the open road, my eyes locked on the horizon. "*I'm mentally preparing for this little Brooklyn adventure. Hope he doesn't scam us to filth.*"

Vonn grinned, still tapping away, he said: "*Well, I was born ready, Mahogany. Pastor Epps better have the cash ready, too, and don't worry; I can vouch for this guy. He's the real deal.*"

The cityscape gave way to the highway, and my determination fueled the drive. Meanwhile, for the rest of the journey, Vonn rapped away, throwing lyrics around like confetti.

"*This is our soundtrack, Mahogany. Brooklyn-bound beats!*" he yelled as he turned up the volume.

As the suburbs transformed into the outskirts of Brooklyn, Vonn and I shared a knowing look, both excited and apprehensive.

"*This is it,*" I said.

Vonn nodded, looking out the window. "*Our stolen gems are about to become Brooklyn's hottest commodity.*"

Brooklyn's energy greeted us like a warm hug; the streets buzzed with life as skyscrapers faded into the background. "Brooklyn, we're ready for you!" I shouted.

The two rolled into the city, the pawn shop's location pinging on the GPS. Vonn, thrilled by the prospect of selling off the jewels, threw in another rap line: "*Brooklyn streets, where stolen dreams turn into cash schemes!*"

I let out a hearty chuckle: "*All right now, save the rhymes for when we actually have the cash in hand, capiche? Let's get these jewels turned into stacks!*"

Finally, the winding road brought us to Pastor Epps' hidden pawn shop on 86th Street in Brooklyn. It was tucked away in a low-key spot, nestled on a quiet one-way street, and few had known that it had a hidden treasure chest inside. Vonn and I exchanged a glance, a silent acknowledgment that we were on the brink of getting the jackpot.

We parked their car on the street and got off, scanning their surroundings. Exiting our '67 super coupe, the Brooklyn Air held a mix of anticipation and a chance at turning fate in our favor. Vonn surveyed the surroundings as we approached the brick storefront that had a weathered sign above the entrance, "*Pastor Epps' Pawn Emporium.*"

"*Huh. I don't remember Pastor Epps' shop being this shady, but then again, the last time I saw him, I was five years old,*" remarked Vonn.

I replied, "*Yeah, a lot's changed since then. Even Brooklyn streets age, you know?*" With mischief dripping from my eyes, I added: "*Ready to turn our stolen goods into Brooklyn gold?*"

Vonn grinned, "*Let's do it, baby. Brooklyn's about to get a whole lot richer – thanks to us.*"

We stepped into the pawn shop, an adventure that awaited us, the air thick with the promise of a unique Brooklyn tale about to unfold. Pushing open the creaking door, a bell chimed softly, announcing our arrival. The interior was faintly lit, casting shadows along the rows of the many items Pastor Epps had displayed in a glass case.

Vonn took a deep breath, his eyes scanning the collection of items from long-gone eras. Pastor Epps, a man with a salt-and-pepper beard and in his late fifties, emerged from a back room. He had a well-built frame, was dressed in a tailored suit, and wanted to give the notion to his customers that he meant business.

With an air of mystery, Pastor swung open the door to greet both of us. Charisma oozed from him, his eyes carrying a mischievous glint as he looked them up and down.

"*Hello! Welcome to Pastor Epps' Pawn Emporium!*" he said as he greeted Vonn and me. "*What can I do for today, for the lovely lady and gentleman?*"

"*Uh, we wanted to exchange some jewels for some cash. You think you can help us out?*" I asked, getting straight to the point. I wasn't in the mood for small talk in the slightest.

"*Pastor Epps, do you remember me? I'm Vonn. I used to come around when I was like, yay, high!*" Vonn gestured with his hand near his leg, palms facing the floor. "*And this is Mahogany, a friend.*" He pointed to me.

"*Vonn! Of course I do, bud. I'm happy to see you; look at you!*" Pastor's eyes sparkled, "*And Mahogany; what a unique name! So, you say you have some jewels for me, eh? Come on, follow me,*" He gestured to us.

I was still skeptical and whispered to Vonn, "*Vonn, I got a feeling this guy doesn't know jack shit. Maybe we should go elsewhere.*"

"*We can't go now; it'll look rude! Besides, he's legit, trust me!*" Vonn replied.

As we stepped through the doorway, Pastor Epps guided us along a lavish hallway adorned with priceless artwork and exquisite antiques. Vonn couldn't help but exchange a glance with me, giving me a suspicious look that meant this wasn't your average pawn shop setup. We eventually reached a shady room, which Pastor Epps called his study.

Pastor Epps, overhearing what I said, turned with a sly grin. "*My dear, looks can be deceiving. Don't judge a book by its cover – especially not in my study.*"

Inside, the shelves were more than a display of knowledge; they were a secret and inconspicuous place to hide money tucked between the pages of those books. It was a covert contingency plan – just in case a swift escape or hefty lawyer's fees were on the agenda.

Vonn, seizing the opportunity to reminisce, chuckled, "*Last time I was here, Pastor, I was still learning to tie my shoes. Loot at us now; we're all grown up with a different kind of business.*"

Pastor Epps grinned, "*Ah, the cycle of life. Now, let's see what treasures you've brought me.*"

I then produced the jewels, with each piece having a unique value of its own. Pastor Epps leaned back in his antique chair and examined them with a connoisseur's eye. 'Old Slick Money Epps,' as he was so famously known, studied the stolen jewels and immediately knew that he had come across a small fortune.

"*Impressive, Mahogany and Vonn. You've got an eye for the finer things,*" he said.

His gaze remained fixed on the diamonds that sparkled from a mile away and the 22-karat gold chain, which particularly captivated him.

Vonn leaned in, "*Well, Pastor, you've got a talent for turning them into cash. What are we talkin' here?*"

"*These jewels speak for themselves, Pastor. Each has its own unique story.*" I remarked while leaning against a bookshelf.

Pastor Epps chuckled: "*Ah, and stories are my favorite kind of currency. Exquisite craftsmanship, I must say.*" he murmured.

His voice was filled with genuine appreciation as he examined the jewels with his rose gold jeweler's loupe. In this elaborate game of risk and reward, we found ourselves now on Pastor Epps' turf — a world where charisma and cunning could turn stolen jewels into the pages of money in hidden books.

His expertise in jewelry shined through as he meticulously inspected the remaining pieces of the stolen treasures — each as marvelous as the last: a dazzling yellow diamond cross and two watches adorned with emeralds and encrusted Rolexes. The weight of each piece felt significant in his hands, and his eyes sparkled with genuine animation. He peered even closer, scrutinizing the diamonds and emeralds with a connoisseur's eye.

Vonn and I exchanged nervous glances as our hopes now hinged on Pastor Epps' judgment and connections. We were well aware of his past business dealings and that his network was vast enough for him to double-cross us and sell the jewels elsewhere for a higher price. At this moment, the stolen jewels were laid bare before a man who could turn their illicit acquisitions into a substantial sum of money.

Pastor Epps continued his examination, revealing a keen eye for the intricacies of each piece, "*You two have stumbled across some treasures!*" he remarked.

His words carried admiration and a sense of rare recognition. It was as if the jewels spoke to him, revealing their stories and actual value. At this point, our nerves tinged with a mixture of excitement and anxiety as we awaited Pastor Epps' judgment. The man's knowledge, evident in the gleam of his eyes and the measured words he spoke, hinted at the possibility of making them both rich beyond their comprehension.

Pastor Epps wore a sly smile that hinted at the confidence he exuded. "*I can handle this for you, my friends. I'll take these off your hands for, let's say... 45 grand!*" his voice oozed with assurance.

The air in the room seemed to thicken with the weight of his words. But there was a caveat—discretion was a non-negotiable. We understood the gravity of the situation and nodded in agreement. Our trust now rested firmly in the hands of the man, who was called Old Slick Money-Making Epps in the streets.

His sly smile hinted at the confidence that had earned him his moniker. As the meeting unfolded, the study transformed into a realm of calculated risk and promised reward. It was like Vonna, and I were now mere players in this intricate game. We watched as our fortunes hung in the balance and suspended between the shadows and the brilliance of the jewels before us.

"*Maybe this guy isn't so bad after all,*" I said to Vonn.

"*You have gotten yourself a deal,*" Vonn said, then shook Pastor Epps' hand and smirked at me; I licked my lips in excitement.

After all was said and done, we went back upstairs to seal the deal when Pastor Epps pulled out his sack of cash with thousands of $20 bills. The thrill was momentarily dampened as Pastor Epps meticulously counted each bill.

Annoyed, I couldn't help but think: "*What the hell is wrong with this guy? He's got a money counter right there. A baby could count faster than him, I swear to God,*" I sighed.

While we waited, I leaned on the glass countertop, looking out the window while the Pastor counted away. It was then that my stomach began to churn with unease when I saw something odd. My eyes widened, spotting a strange blue work van seemingly surveilling the store, but I resisted alarming Vonn and Pastor Epps.

"*Come on, get a move on,*" I whispered urgently, signaling to Vonn and Epps.

"*Okay, okay, geez!*" replied Vonn.

After Pastor was done counting, Vonn swiftly stashed the money in a backpack, "*Pleasure doin' business with you, Pastor!*" Vonn said, shooting Epps a smile, and headed toward the door.

"*I told you; this guy doesn't toy about. Think about it, Mahogany. These jewels could be our ticket to freakin' $45,000 – enough to wipe out our problems and start fresh!*" Vonn whispered to me as I darted out of the store.

As we headed out, Vonn's eyes widened as he caught sight of that very blue van parked across the street, but he didn't think anything of it, from what I could tell. We flung the door open, making a beeline for their Chevy, and peeled out of there as fast as we could.

***

As the sun began to set, the trio got down to some secret severe negotiations and tricky transactions. Their journey took a turn into this clandestine world that had a mix of excitement and a vibe they'd only caught glimpses of before. Pastor Epps, the mastermind behind this sneaky game, moved with the smoothness of someone who's been there and done that.

Clandestine negotiations, the hush-hush moves in the shadows – it was all adding to changing the fortunes of everyone in that pawn shop. The trio were now on the same wavelength and diving into a maze of secrets and potential payoffs, riding on the charm and finesse of the guy who earned himself the title of Slick Money-Making Epps.

As the sun said its goodbyes, casting longer shadows around the room, those stolen jewels became more than just shiny pieces of refined rocks. They were the keys to a future where the headaches of the salon were a thing of the past. The dollar bills were just pieces of paper, and life got a bit more straightforward. The trio, now a tight crew with a shared mission, waded further into the intricate negotiations with Pastor Epps. Their destinies were hanging in the balance, ready for a plot twist that could change the trajectory of their lives.

***

Soon, the reality of what we had done began to sink in. As we drove off, my mind was a tornado of emotions. I understood that the repercussions of our actions would echo far beyond this moment and grappled with the weight of my choices.

All I could think about at the moment was: *"What would my parents think of me, and what have I done?"*

I looked over to Vonn, who looked like a man firm in his decision. He had no remorse; as long as it made me happy, it didn't matter to him.

Along the drive, Vonn revealed to me what Pastor Epps had whispered to him: "*Guess what happened back in there. Pastor Epps asked if we could do some more burglaries for him.*"

"*Hell, no!*" I yelled.

"*The nerve of that guy! Ugh, I need to go to the bathroom; make a stop around here, would you?*"

We stopped at the Burger Metropolis, after which I stepped out of the car and looked back at Vonn.

"*Get it out of your mind about doing anything with that slick-ass Epps. Got it?*" I told him.

"*You're the boss,*" Vonn winked. "*One more thing; don't put your half of the money in the bank. We'll use money orders.*"

The rest of the ride back home was long, and the road seemed winding. Gosh, I couldn't wait to get home; I just needed to wash the day off in a steaming hot shower and dream about my bed. On the drive back, I sat in silence, my mind consumed by the events of the day. I knew that I couldn't ignore the gravity of my choices any longer.

Epilogue

With the cash in hand, I stood at the crossroads of my life, burdened by the weight of the choices I had made thus far. The blue van had come and gone, and Pastor Epps had handed Vonn and me the bag filled with $45,000 – a bag that now weighed heavier than ever on me, with the consequences of our actions.

To make matters more complicated, the police were still on the hunt and were closing in on me with each passing minute. On the drive home, the engine roared to life, and we left the city's chaotic landscape behind. Things changed when we got a tip from Nicole that the police had raided the salon, and it dawned on me: I could never go back there, even if I wanted to.

Vonn, blissfully unaware of the turmoil brewing within me, drove across the country back to the place I once called my home. My mind was thrust into a storm of conflicting emotions. The decision I had to make loomed over me like a storm cloud – one that would alter the course of my life forever.

Vonn, on the opposite end of the spectrum, reveled in the excitement of our newfound wealth, "*All this dough...Mahogany, baby, we're gonna live like kings and queens!*"

But I knew I had reached the point of no return. Without a word, I asked Vonn to stop the car. I got out of the Chevy, which had been our getaway vehicle, but now was a desperate bid for my freedom, and I could feel the weight of the stolen money pressing against me on my chest.

The crisp bills were a symbol of both escape and entrapment. The city lights blurred into streaks of neon as we raced against the approaching storm, one that was a long time coming. We were in a secluded spot, and the realization struck me like a lightning bolt — I couldn't bring Vonn along on the journey that my life was now on.

Our lives had become intertwined in the pursuit of quick gains and dangerous thrills, but the consequences were catching up to us, and that too at an alarming speed. With a heavy heart, I made a choice that would sever all the ties to my past. As I stepped out of that car, I felt the weight of the bag of money in my hands; it suddenly became too heavy for me.

"*Oh, Vonn, I hope you'll understand. I don't want to...God knows I don't want to. The police are after me...they'll never stop looking for me. I want to stop running. I have to leave. I have to leave.*"

"*Mahogany? Get back in the car! We gotta go!*" Vonn urged me.

"*I can't!*" I told him.

This would be the last moment that we shared, together. I debated on whether or not I should tell him what I had reluctantly prepared to do. After much deliberation, I decided that I had to tell Vonn; I owed him this much, at least.

I could feel the city's pulse vibrating through the cracked pavement. I could feel the urgency of my parting ways with this city and with everyone I knew. I then turned to Vonn, who was still reveling in the adrenaline of our escape, with tears in my eyes, and broke the news to him:

"*Vonn,*" I said, my voice breaking with resolution and regret. He got out of the car and walked towards me, his eyes reflecting the glow of the city lights.

"*I need you to do something for me.*"

"*Anything, Mahogany!*" Vonn replied, his excitement undiminished but his confusion apparent.

I hesitated, a pang of guilt tugging at me. "*I... I need you to go back. To your life, your people. Forget about me.*"

Vonn's face contorted in confusion. "*What are you talking about? We did it, Mahogany! We got the money. We're free!*"

"*No, Vonn,*" I said, my eyes welling up. "*I need to be free. Like truly free. And that means leaving everything behind. Including you.*"

His eyes widened in disbelief. "*You're...leaving? Without me?*"

"*I have to, Vonn,*" I whispered. "*This isn't a life I can share with anyone. The police are closing in, and I can't drag you down with me.*"

Vonn, grappling with the sudden revelation, stepped back. "*You're just gonna disappear? After everything?*"

At this point, I was a wreck, but I held my ground. "*I have to, Vonn. For both of us.*"

He shook his head, and I saw anger and sadness in his eyes. "*You can't just decide this on your own. We're a team, Mahogany.*" He held my hands in his, and I slowly receded.

I placed a hand on his cheek, a bittersweet smile on my lips. "*Not anymore, Vonn. I have to go. Here,*" I tossed him the bag of cash, "*Take this off my hands, will ya?*"

The city lights flickered and cast shadows on his face as I looked back at Vonn. "*Take care of yourself!*" I whispered, and it felt like the city's whispers carried my voice away.

Leaving behind it all, I walked away, my decision becoming more and more accurate with every step. I looked back at Vonn one last time in a silent farewell and left. With each step, I left behind everything and everyone — the stolen jewels, the money, my salon, Nicole, Vonn, and the shadows of my past.

It was like the city had swallowed me, and I became a phantom, vanishing into the sea of faces. The place seemed to echo with the fading sound of the Chevy, leaving Vonn standing alone, grappling with the reality that I — Mahogany, his partner in crime — had vanished without a trace. A haunting realization enveloped me: sometimes, choices are made in the shadows that forever alter the course of partnerships and the lives we once shared.

Before I left for an unknown destination, I needed to do one last thing: I had to tell Nicole. I wrote her a letter and mailed it to her with a heavy heart. I read as follows:

Dear Nicole,

By the time you read this, I'll be gone. The path that my life is on, I have to face it by myself.

I want you to know that our friendship meant the world to me. You were there in the late nights at the salon, sharing stories and secrets. We laughed, we cried, and did some crazy shit. And that, I'll never forget.

I can't ask you to understand the reasons for my decision to leave. Sometimes, the shadows we create engulf us, and we find ourselves lost within them. The stolen jewels, the heists, and the life of crime that I lived – all have led me to the point of no return. I need to break free from this, and the only way is to disappear. Please don't ask me where, because I don't know myself.

Vonn doesn't know about this letter. The burden of my choices is mine to bear, and I won't drag him down with me. I trust that he will find his way like he always does.

Please take care of yourself, Nicole. Take care of the salon. I want you to remember the good times we shared.

Our paths may never cross again, but I'll carry the memories of our friendship with me.

Yours always, Mahogany.

And with that, I took what little money I had and went to the train station, bidding farewell to everything I once held near and dear. I didn't know where I was going, and I was terrified. But, deep in my heart, I knew it was the right thing to do. And so, off I went, searching for a fresh start and a new place to call home.

Made in the USA
Columbia, SC
18 March 2025

55327597R00063